Captain Felonius

Written by Joy Cowley
Illustrated by Elizabeth Fuller

There was a pirate called Captain Felonius
who had a very bad temper. When something upset him,
he would shout at the top of his voice.

What terrible words he used!

When he began to swear, his crew put their hands over
their ears. Sea gulls screamed and flew away from the ship.
The cat ran up the mast.

"Now see here, my dearie-o," said Mrs. Felonius.
"Your swearing is really terrible. Why don't you give it up?"

"I can't," said the Captain. "Sorry, my little flower,
but I just can't help it."

And he went on swearing.

One day the crew stopped work. They sat down
on the deck, and the First Mate said, "Captain,
you're always calling us bad names. We're sick of it.
No more swearing, or we go on strike."

At once, Captain Felonius flew into a rage.
He ran to his cabin, shut the door,
and shouted all the swearwords he knew.

"Tut, tut, my dearie-o!" said Mrs. Felonius.

The Captain told her what the First Mate had said. "My crew is going to mutiny!" he cried.

"But I can't stop swearing. I have tried. I just can't help it."

"I've got an idea," said his wife. "Every time you want to swear, come down to your cabin. Write the swearword on a piece of paper. Put it in your old chest. Then go back to your crew."

The Captain hugged his wife. "What a clever little flower you are," he said. "What would I do without you?"

He went up on deck and said to his crew, "All right.
I give you my word. I won't swear at you again."

"Bet you will," said the First Mate.

"Promise, I won't," said the Captain.

"You will," said the First Mate.

"I won't! I won't!" yelled the Captain, getting red in the face.

"Will, will, will!" the First Mate laughed.

The Captain shook with anger.
"Don't talk to me like that, you—you—"

His hand went over his mouth. He ran to his cabin
and got a pen and paper.

He wrote down a very bad word. It was so bad,
it made the paper turn brown and curl like thin toast.

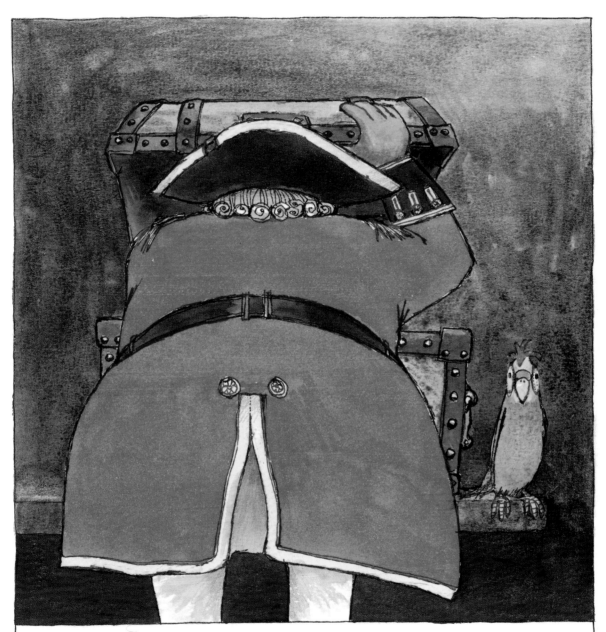

He put the swearword in the old chest.
Then he went back to his crew and smiled at the First Mate.
"See?" he said.

After that, the Captain put all his swearwords on paper. When something upset him, down to the cabin he'd go. Out would come the pen and paper. Into the chest would go the swearword.

For three days a storm shook the ship. The rain ran down the Captain's back. Salt water filled his boots. The Captain shook his fist at the sea and stamped his wet boots. How he wanted to swear! But always he put his hand over his mouth and ran to the cabin.

The mast broke in the storm.
Down to the cabin went the Captain.
The sail got ripped. The rigging was tangled.
The Captain ran down to the cabin.

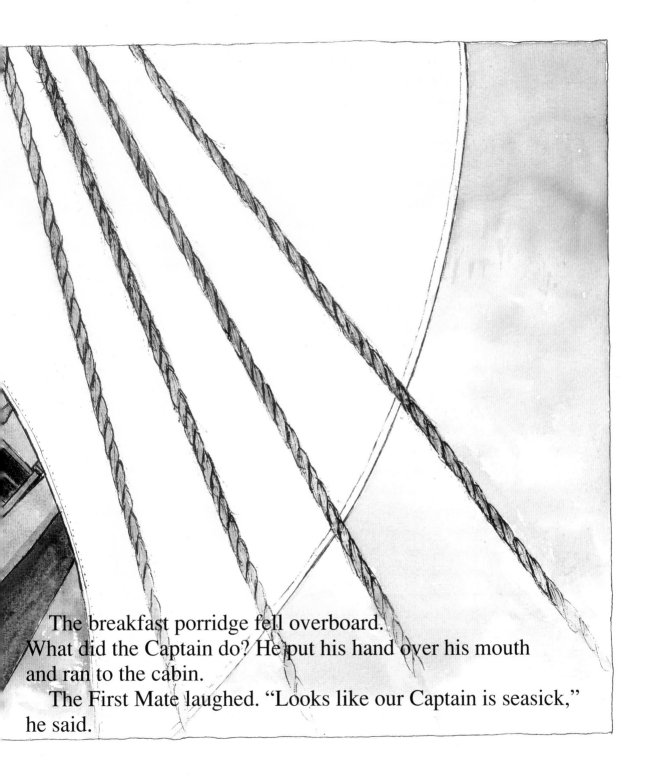

The breakfast porridge fell overboard.
What did the Captain do? He put his hand over his mouth and ran to the cabin.

The First Mate laughed. "Looks like our Captain is seasick," he said.

When the storm was over, the chest was full of paper. Not one more word could go in it. The Captain put his ear against the chest. Inside, there was a humming like electricity.

He said to his wife, "It sounds dangerous. I should get rid of it."

"Why don't you bury it?" she said.

"A good idea, my little flower," said the Captain. "We're very close to an island. I'll row there tonight when the crew are asleep. I'll bury the chest where no one can find it."

That night when all was quiet, the Captain put the chest in the rowboat. He went to the island and made a hole under a tree. He put the chest in; then he filled up the hole.

"No one will know it's here," he said.

But the First Mate had seen him. The First Mate had been watching with greedy eyes.

"Ha!" he said. "So that's what he's up to!" And he woke the other pirates.

"Treasure!" he said. "That's what it is. Treasure! Our Captain's playing a dirty trick on us. He wants to hide it all for himself."

The crew got dressed, and they rowed to the island.
It was easy to see where the Captain had been digging.
The pirates uncovered the chest and dragged it from the hole.
They all stood around it.
"Full of gold, I'll bet," said the First Mate.
"Open it! Open it!" cried the others.
"Here goes!" said the First Mate, and he pulled up the lid.

What a shock he got! Out came the pieces of
paper, humming like mad bees.

They flew at the First Mate and stung him on his ears.
Then they stung the other pirates.

There were pieces of paper everywhere, humming and stinging.
The pirates put their hands over their ears. They ran
for the rowboat. They bumped into each other and fell.
They screamed and shouted terrible words,
as the pieces of paper followed them.

Over on the ship, Captain Felonius was trying
to see the island. He called to his wife.
"Can you hear that noise, my little flower?" he asked.
"What is it, my dearie-o?" she said.
"My crew," said Captain Felonius. "They're on the island.
They've been looking for treasure."

"Treasure?" said Mrs. Felonius. "Then why are they shouting ose terrible words?"

Captain Felonius smiled. "I don't know," he said. "Maybe they just can't help it."